SOUP IN THE SADDLE

SOUP in the SADDLE

by ROBERT NEWTON PECK

Illustrated by Charles Robinson

A YEARLING BOOK

Published by
Dell Publishing
a division of
Bantam Doubleday Dell Publishing Group, Inc.
666 Fifth Avenue
New York, New York 10103

ISBN: 0-440-40032-5

Reprinted by arrangement with Alfred A. Knopf, Inc.

Printed in the United States of America

January 1988

10 9 8 7 6 5 4 3

CW

*To Frances Foster,
my loyal and faithful editor,
who, when I don't write good,
gives me swell adjectives.*

SOUP IN THE SADDLE

"Higher," said Soup.

"It's no use," I said, looking down at him. "We're just going to have to add one more barrel."

Soup was safe on the ground. But I was standing on a trembling stack of four apple barrels, trying to reach the second-floor window of the old red barn.

"Try jumping," Soup told me.

"I'll fall and bust my butt."

Soup scratched his neck. From up where I was clinging to a loose board, I could see that my pal, Luther Vinson, was urging his brain into a higher gear.

"I'm climbing down," I said.

"No," said Soup, "I'm climbing up."

"You best not do it, Soup. This stack of barrels is already shaking enough with just me up here."

"Don't worry, Rob. I'm half steeplejack."

As I felt the pile of barrels shake even worse, I wanted to tell Soup that his other half was jackass. It wouldn't help. Soup had earlier said that he'd heard there was a big surprise up in the loft of this old deserted barn.

Up he came.

Our tall column of barrels felt as if they didn't want to play a part in Soup's crazy idea any more than I did.

"Ya know," I told Soup as he struggled upward, "my mother told me that we weren't ever supposed to go near this old barn. Because the wood's near rotten and it's fixing to tumble down."

"That's funny," said Soup. "My mother told me the very same thing."

"And worse yet, if old Mr. McGinley catches us here, trying to sneak in a window, then heck won't hold all the trouble we'll be in."

"He won't catch us," said Soup.

My hands were starting to cramp up as I was holding the loose board real tight. Even tighter when I felt Soup's fingers grab the back of my pants.

"Easy," I said. "I forgot my belt this morning. You're pulling my pants down."

"Sometimes," said Soup, "stuff's got to come down so that other stuff can climb up."

With a final grunt, he made it. Both of us were now huddled on the top barrel. Even though Soup was two inches taller than I was, his fingertips couldn't quite reach the sill of the window.

"I told ya, Soup."

"Rob, old top, there's only one thing to do."

"Get down?"

"No, not quite. We're almost home free. All we need now is one more barrel. Just one more."

"If we're *both* up here, how do you expect we can get a fifth barrel?"

Soup grinned at me. "You're it."

"Me?"

"Right. Rob, old top, *you're* our extra barrel. So all I do now is just skin up your back. Give me a boost."

"A *boost?* All I can do is hang on. These barrels are going over, Soup. I can near to feel myself falling."

"If there's anything I can't abide," said Soup, "it's a quitter."

"Okay," I said. Nobody was going to call Robert Peck a quitter, I was thinking. Only a fool.

"Hold still and I'll be up on your shoulders before you even know I'm there."

As I held on, up Soup went. He must have put on some pounds because it felt like he weighed close to two hundred. And the soles of his bare feet were really biting into my shoulders on both sides of my neck. His toes didn't smell like roses. It was plain to the nose on my face that Soup and I had come to the barn by way of Mr. Cyrus McGinley's cow pasture.

"Steady," said Soup.

As he said it more like a grunt, I knew that Soup was wrestling with the window. I heard a squeak, then a long squeal, sounding as though he'd finally pushed open the dirty old window. As he gave the final nudge, it felt to me as if my shoulders were holding up all of Vermont.

"Can you see anything in there, Soup?"

"It's sort of dark. But now I see something."

"Like what?" I asked him.

"Hornets." Soup was quiet for a few seconds so I figured he was up to more thinking. He was. "Rob, maybe it would be a good idea if *you* went in first."

"Why *me?* You're up there and I'm down here."

Soup sighed. "We could swap places. You're plenty lighter than I am, which means I could push you in right easy."

"Doggone it, Soup," I grunted. "You're getting too heavy to argue with. This whole mess was *your* idea, not mine. My hands hurt and my bare feet are standing on a splinter."

"Okay, hang on."

As he sudden felt lighter, I knew he was climbing in the window. Looking up, I saw nothing of him at all; only a black square of dust and darkness where the window had been. Then I heard him yell.

"Rob! It's *here!*"

"Swell. What is it?"

"Just wait'll you see. And it's about the biggest one I ever laid eyes on. And real old."

I couldn't wait. "Soup, I'm climbing in, too. Reach out and gimme a hand up."

"No," said Soup. "Here it comes."

Next thing I heard was a dull scrape of a sound telling me that whatever *it* was, Luther Vinson was dragging it closer and closer to the window. Soup was grunting on every yank.

"What is it, Soup? I gotta know."

"You'll see."

"Why can't you tell me? It sure isn't any fun out here, standing on this dumb old barrel. You're having all the sport of it while I'm just a ladder."

I heard one more drag. "It's a surprise," said Soup. "You won't believe what we found."

"No," I said, "I probable won't. Whatever it is, we can't steal it, Soup. Because it belongs to Mr. McGinley."

Soup was panting. The item that he was tugging on must have been powerful hefty. Or nailed down.

"Nobody," said Soup, "mentioned anything about stealing. All we're going to do is sort of *borrow* it. Then we'll bring it right back."

I smelled trouble. And it was a stronger stink than Soup's feet. Again I heard Mama's warning voice ... to stay away from Mr. McGinley's old barn. Why hadn't I heeded her advice? Maybe she knew things I didn't know and was getting to be a whole lot smarter than even Soup.

"Okay," grunted Soup. "Here she be."

Looking up, I saw a giant hunk of brown something that was being pushed out the window. Part of it looked like a blanket, all gray. A strap dangled over the ledge of the window and hung down toward my hand.

"Grab it," Soup told me.

With extreme care, fearful that the stack of barrels I stood on were fixing to topple over and spill, I reached up a timid hand. My fingers took a firm purchase on the black strap.

"I got it, Soup."

"Good. Okay, you pull and I'll push."

"But if'n it's heavy in there, it'll be even a whole lot heftier out here."

"Don't worry," Soup told me. "But now ya gotta pull a lot harder because she's stuck in the window."

I yanked my strap. Yet nothing happened.

"Okay," said Soup. "On the count of three, I'll heave my shoulder to her and you *yank.*"

"I'll fall."

"No, you won't. Because as soon as we budge 'er out the window, I'll hold tight from up here. But first, I'll back up and get a running start. Ready?"

"Well, sort of."

"Here goes," said Soup. "One. Two. *Three!*"

I yanked. My tug on the strap was so hard that it lifted both my feet up off the top barrel. It worked. Whatever the surprise was, out it came. It was big, heavy, and moving. But it didn't come out through the window alone.

Soup came too.

He let out a scream. "Hornets!" In less than a second, I was holding the big surprise on top of which was Soup. It was all too much for anybody my size to hold. My tower of barrels underneath must have shared the same opinion.

We toppled.

Down we fell. Besides me, there came four barrels, Soup, and his big surprise. Closing my eyes, I prepared to die. When I hit the mud below, Vermont sure felt hard enough. But when Soup landed, on me, everything felt a whole bit harder. Even though I hurt all over, I opened my eyes to see bouncing barrels, stars, and Soup's big surprise. I couldn't believe what I saw.

A cowboy saddle.

2

"*Yahoo!*" yelled Soup.

I was lying in the mud. On top of me was a blanket plus a big saddle which Soup was pretending to ride like a cowboy.

"Get off," I said, groaning.

Soup got up slowly. "We did it, Rob. By golly, Ally Tidwell was *right*. He said he'd spotted an old saddle up in Mr. McGinley's barn. But we're the lucky ones because *we* get to borrow it first."

I was too scared to move.

Every bone in my body, I was sure, must be busted in at least a hundred places. Cowboys, according to Soup, always wanted to die in the saddle. Here I was, dying underneath Mr. McGinley's.

"Pull it off me, Soup. I can't breathe."

With a grunt, Soup lugged the saddle off me, but I couldn't get up. With a careful finger, I tried to pry a hunk of mud out of one ear. Everywhere I looked I saw barrels.

Soup stood beside the saddle with a big grin spreading across his freckles. "Rob," he said, "at last our dreams are about to come true."

I moaned.

Soup knelt down and slapped the saddle. "At last we get a chance to become real cowboys. All we need to borrow now is just one more thing."

"One more thing?" I asked.

"A horse."

Hearing him say it made me hurt even worse. I didn't need a horse. What I needed was either a hospital or an undertaker. Yet, as I slowly got to my hands and knees and looked at the saddle, the thought of finally becoming a genuine cowboy made me feel a tickle happier.

But then I looked up at the open window of the red barn. It seemed to be at least a mile up.

"Soup," I asked, "now that we've borrowed our saddle, how are we ever going to get it back through that window up there?"

"Don't worry," Soup told me. "We'll tackle that job later. We sure aren't going to waste a Saturday fretting on tiny problems, are we?"

"No," I said, struggling to my feet, "I don't guess we are."

Soup smiled. "That's the spirit."

I stared down at the cowboy saddle. "But what if Mr. McGinley finds out we . . . *borrowed* it?"

I could see that Soup wasn't listening. The expression on his face told me that, once again, his brain was cranking, which could lead to only one end. More trouble. My backside still hurt. And it would hurt ample more if my folks ever found out what Soup and I were up to.

"Rob, I've got him all picked out."

"Who?"

"Our horse."

I looked blankly at Soup before I could say anything. "But neither one of us knows how to be a cowboy. All we ever do is see a cowboy movie at the picture show. Then you pretend you're Tom Mix and I'm Buck Jones."

"So?"

"We just run and slap our hips. But that's only make-believe. We're not cowboys, Soup. All we are is saddle rustlers. And when old McGinley catches us . . ."

"Come on," said Soup. "Let's grab our saddle and hightail it over to the meadow where I saw the horse."

Soup grabbed the light end of the saddle and I was too weak to argue. As we lifted it up on my shoulders, I don't guess I ever realized that one saddle could weigh more than one horse. Soup and his crazy ideas. I was now carrying the saddle while Soup toted the blanket.

"How far is this horse of yours?"

"Not very far," said Soup.

Soup was wrong.

By the time I carried the saddle as far as the meadow fence, I knew I was at least a year older and ten years dumber. Soup, however, seemed to appear even more spirited. As I flopped the big cowboy saddle across the top rail of the fence, Soup pointed.

"There he is."

Sure enough, there he was. A big black horse slowly walking our way. *Never,* my mother had always warned me, cut through a pasture. But as the horse plodded closer and closer, he sure didn't look too ugly or dangerous.

Reaching into his pocket, Soup smiled. He pulled out a carrot which he waved to the horse.

"His name's Gentle George," said Soup.

"How do you know?"

Soup grinned. "I just named him. He's real gentle. See how slow he's walking. But once we're up on his back, I bet he can really gallop."

Soup held the carrot on the flat of his hand. George sniffed at it and then lipped it into his mouth. I could hear his teeth munching it down. Once again, Soup reached into his pocket.

"Okay," he said, "while I feed him one more carrot, you throw the blanket and saddle over his back."

"Me? It's too heavy."

"You want to be a cowboy, don't you?"

I nodded. I did want to be a cowboy. So I tossed the blanket onto Gentle George's broad back and then attempted to do the same with the saddle. "Aren't you going to help, Soup?"

"Sure," he said. "I'm handling the carrot."

How I hefted a ton of saddle over the fence and onto George I'll never know. Yet I did it. Soup squinted.

"Rob, are you sure the saddle horn is supposed to be in back? It just don't look proper."

Soup was right. The saddle didn't look proper to me either. But I told Soup that I didn't have enough strength left in me to right it around.

"Okay," said Soup. "It doesn't matter. Tighten the belly strap and we'll climb aboard old George here and ride the range."

Wow, I was thinking as I worked the strap through the ring under the saddle flap, this was going to be fun. I could hardly wait. Gentle George just stood there, gently, living up to his name. He sure was a friendly animal.

"You get on first," said Soup.

"Why me?"

"Because you're lighter."

What Soup was saying didn't total up to a whole bag of sense, but I was far too eager to put up a fuss. Not when I was about to be, for the first time in my life, a cowboy.

Up I went.

Gentle George stood still. As my leg swung up over his back and into the saddle, our big black horse never even twitched.

"Come on, Soup. Climb aboard."

"Okay, I'm just waiting to see if Gentle George

is planning to do something."

"Like what?"

"Buck."

Hearing what Soup said made me reach behind my back to grab the horn of the saddle and fast. But it seemed we had little to fear. George was as gentle as he was big. Still and all, I noticed how cautious Soup was when he finally vaulted up into the saddle behind me.

"How come I'm in front, Soup?"

His answer did not come in words. All he did was put his arms around my waist and hang on.

"Okay," said Soup, "kick his ribs."

"No," I said. "Gentle George didn't kick me so why should I kick him?" After I said that I spoke just one word to Gentle George. "Giddyap."

George didn't budge.

"We're not galloping very fast," said Soup.

He was right. Gentle George was standing in the same spot and didn't lift a hoof. Not even when I urged his ribs with my heels. I clucked out a "giddyap" a few more times, yet nothing seemed to work. George was a statue.

"Hey! You boys!"

The voice almost froze my blood. Behind me, I felt Soup wince and his arms tightened more than a mite. Turning, I saw a man coming our way and he sure didn't look too happy.

"Remember," whispered Soup, "*you* got on first."

The man walked over to the fence, reached over, and clutched the hair of Gentle George's mane. I knew who he was. His name was Mr. Carlotta.

"Now," he told us, "I don't want you boys to panic. One at a time, I want you to climb off that horse, very slowly."

Soup, I noticed, climbed off first. He wasted no time doing it. Not a wink. I climbed off too. I thought Mr. Carolotta was going to be really sore, yet he wasn't. His voice was soft and steady.

"Is he *your* horse, Mr. Carlotta?" I asked.

"Yes. He's mine."

"We weren't hurting him," Soup said. "Honest."

Mr. Carlotta said, "I believe it. You're just lucky he didn't hurt *you*. He's a racehorse, or used to be. I've put him out to stud. You lads don't realize what a close call you just escaped from."

I couldn't believe what I was hearing. "But he's real gentle, Mr. Carlotta. Honest he is. Soup and I didn't know his name, so we were calling him Gentle George."

Mr. Carlotta looked at the old saddle, shook his head, and smiled.

"Boys," he said, "his name isn't Gentle George. Would you like to know his real name?"

Soup and I both nodded.

"Thunderbolt."

3

Monday morning came.

Soup and I, plus all the rest of our class, were in our seats. Miss Kelly stood at our big wall map holding a pointer and tapping its tip near the center of Asia.

"And this country," she said, "is called . . ."

"Mexico," said Janice Riker.

Miss Kelly sighed. Janice, I knew, was not our teacher's favorite kid. Nor was she mine. Janice

Riker may have owned the smallest brain in the room; yet she also cocked the biggest fist, with the meanest temper. Her number-one sport was boxing and I was her favorite punching bag.

"I'm sure," said Miss Kelly in her patient voice, "that what Janice meant to say was Mongolia."

"That's funny," said Janice. "Because right out in front of our house we got a tree called a Mongolia."

Soup giggled. But then he turned off quiet when Miss Kelly shot him one of her warning glances. Over her glasses. It was one of her many tricks to skirt trouble before it got hatched.

"Your tree," said Miss Kelly to Janice, "I believe, is a *magnolia*. However, what we're learning about this morning is Mongolia, a country known for its barren land. And for fast horses."

Soup and I looked at each other. I figured he was thinking about the very same horse that I was remembering. Thunderbolt.

Outside, a car honked.

It was a sound we'd heard for years. The car was a tiny Hoover. Yet, we knew, its driver was not tiny at all. Laying down her pointer, Miss Kelly opened the door. In walked our visitor, smiling.

"Howdy, kids!"

"Good morning, Miss Boland," we all chorused.

Our caller was our county nurse, all dressed in white and wearing a big grin on an even bigger face. I smiled, too. So did Soup, because whenever Miss Boland popped in, it usually spelled *news.*

"We *did* it," Miss Boland announced, her enormous body almost shaking with excitement. Out of breath, Miss Boland flopped herself down on the edge of Miss Kelly's desk and wheezed.

Miss Kelly smiled. "Please tell us what you're up to. I can tell something's afoot."

"Sure is." Miss Boland smacked her open hand with her other fist. "I just came from a School Board meeting. And we're all set. Believe *me,*" she said, gasping for air, "they were all dead set against it."

"That," said Miss Kelly, "I believe."

"But," said Miss Boland, *"I* talked them into it."

"I'm sure you did."

Miss Boland skipped to her feet. "Guess what? Next week, we're going to have . . ." She paused to look at our teacher. "I really shouldn't tell, you know."

Miss Kelly nodded. "Yet I'm confident you will."

"I can't hold back a second longer. We're throwing a special day, next Wednesday, so listen up, you kids . . . there's going to be . . . *no school!*"

We all cheered.

"Wait!" Miss Boland held up her chubby hands. "There's more. I have decided . . . along with the other board members, that next Wednesday is going to be officially declared as . . ." She stopped again to look at Miss Kelly. "Darn gum it, I never could keep a secret."

"Well, for someone who can't," said Miss Kelly, "I'd say that you're certainly doing an excellent job."

"Wednesday's going to be . . . *Miss Kelly Day!*"

Everyone was quiet. The only sudden sound I heard was when our teacher dropped her piece of chalk. It hit the floor, silently rolled beneath her desk, and lay there.

"But why?" asked Miss Kelly.

Miss Boland snorted. "Why indeed. In case you're too feeble to recall, next Wednesday's your birthday. Not only that, this spring marks thirty years you've served as a schoolmarm here in Learning."

I saw Miss Kelly stretch out a hand to touch the wall, as if she was near leaning to hold herself erect.

"So I told the board," said Miss Boland, "that

it's high time you had yourself a day off. Not to mention," she said, looking at us, "a day off school for this herd of young rascals."

Striding over to our open window, Miss Boland stuck out her head, looked at the sky, and popped back inside again. "I sure hope and pray the weather holds. And if it rains, I'll never go to church for at least a year."

Soup nudged me. "No school. Maybe, after chores, we can go fishing or something?"

"Okay," I said. "Or maybe ride the range."

"Now, you youngsters," said Miss Boland, "don't think we're leaving any of *you* out of the celebration. I just made a few long-distance telephone calls, and we're inviting a brass band over to parade up Main Street."

"I can't believe all this," Miss Kelly said.

"Believe it. Thirty years is a long term in this old firetrap, and by golly, we're going to honor you proper. But, you're really not supposed to know."

Norma Jean Bissell raised her hand with a beautiful and graceful gesture. I sighed. Soup noticed my doing it and pretended he was going to throw up.

"Miss Boland," asked Norma Jean, "who else besides the brass band is coming to town?"

Our county nurse began to count on her fingers. "One, the band. Two, we're having a picnic in the park and a balloon vendor is coming. And three, a very special guest is coming to sing and play a guitar."

"Who?" we all asked.

I saw Miss Boland's smile broaden. "No other," she told us, "than Vermont's favorite singing cowboy himself, Mr. Hoot Holler."

On that note, even Miss Kelly clapped her hands. Wow! I couldn't believe what I was hearing. The most famous cowboy in all of Vermont was actually coming to Learning. There wasn't a kid in the entire county who hadn't heard Hoot Holler's metallic notes and his nasal wail.

Hoot's most recent hit song, "Pajamas and Spurs," got played over the radio almost every week.

That was when Soup raised his hand. "Miss Boland, is Hoot Holler going to come to town on his horse?"

Miss Boland slapped her hip with a quick draw of an imaginary six-gun. "You *bet* he is. His horse, lasso, both six-shooters, and, of course, his silver guitar."

I could see that even Soup was impressed with the news. "Maybe," he whispered to me, "we'll save fishing for a later date."

"Sure thing," I said. "We dont want to miss our only chance in a lifetime to actually meet Hoot Holler and hear him sing."

"We certain don't," Soup added.

Up front, I saw that Miss Boland was waving her arms once again, in an effort to settle us all down. "That's not all," she said when we were finally quiet enough to listen up. "I've got one more surprise. And this one is just for your teacher."

It was Miss Kelly's turn to be impressed. "A special surprise just for *me?*"

"Right," said Miss Boland.

"Is it Hoot?" asked Janice.

Several of the kids moaned. Janice Riker, I was thinking, didn't seem to be following all the news that Miss Boland was trying her best to tell us.

"I wish Janice would shut up," Soup said.

"Good idea," I said. "Why don't you tell her to?"

"Not me," said Soup. "I like living."

Miss Kelly spotted the two of us whispering and fired us her be-quiet-or-be-sorry look. Then she turned to Miss Boland in order to learn more about her very special surprise.

"Years ago," said Miss Boland to all of us, "back in days when your teacher and I were young flappers, we used to go to school with a very bright girl. And she's coming, too, next Wednesday."

"A *girl?*" Soup asked her.

"Well now," Miss Boland went on to explain, "needless to say, she isn't a girl *today*. She's a grown-up lady. In fact, you *might* even go so far as to say that, here in Vermont, she's darn near as famous as Mr. Hoot Holler."

Who, I was wondering, could be more famous than Hoot? Nobody I could think of. Miss Boland sure had a hot secret up her white sleeve.

"Her name," said Miss Boland, "is Agatha Jones, and she's a long-time friend of mine as well as Miss Kelly's."

Looking at our teacher, I saw Miss Kelly smile. "My," she said, "I haven't heard from Agatha in years. Isn't she living up in Burlington?"

"No," said Miss Boland, with a firm shake of her head. "Not up there. She's coming to Learning from her new residence, all the way from the city that's the state capital of Vermont."

"And," added Miss Kelly rather proudly, turning to us, "you children all know the name of our state capital." She paused, waiting. "It's spelled M-O-N . . ."

"Mongolia!" yelled Janice.

4

School was over.

Soup and I, as soon as we had outrun Janice, a feat that daily saved our lives, pulled up short for purposes of panting.

A week ago, both Soup and I had committed a critical error. Janice had bent over, in school, to pick up her pencil. As she stooped, Soup and I made a disgusting noise. This, I also well recalled, had displeased Miss Kelly, who then had ordered us both to stay after school.

As we finally left the little red brick building, there was Janice, her face redder than the reddest brick. And both fists a lot harder. It was a bloody fight, spilling mostly Soup's blood and mine. Worse yet, it was shameful for us to admit that a *girl* could tackle the pair of us and then uncle us down.

Soup leaned against a fence and puffed.

"Rob, if I live to be a hundred years old, there's a girl I now go to school with that I'll never forget."

I knew he meant Janice Riker. As for me, the girl I could never forget was Norma Jean Bissell. I actual adored her far more than I worshipped Hoot Holler. This, however, was a sentiment I *wasn't* about to share with Soup. His nose was still a mite puffy as a result of last week's tangle with Janice.

"I know what you're thinking," said Soup.

"Betcha don't."

"Any time you get that sick look on your face, it means one of two things. Either your lunch milk was sour or you're mooning over Norma Jean Bissell like a sick calf. So, which one is it?"

"Milk," I lied.

It was a hot day so we both shucked off our socks and sneakers.

"I don't believe it," said Soup. "You know, unless you're careful, you could wind up as only a husband. Then you'd be saddled to Norma Jean *Peck* for the rest of your life. Or worse, you'd turn into being just a Robert Newton Bissell."

"Right," I said, thinking secretly of what a paradise it would be. But not like the Paradise Diner down near the paper mill. Norma Jean was several shades cleaner.

Soup hopped up to sit on the top rail of the fence. He shook a finger toward my face.

"Once you're married, fun's over. Guys who get wed don't *ever* get to be cowboys. All you'll get for a lasso will be the one Norma Jean throws around your neck. For *keeps*."

I sat beside Soup. "Well," I told him, "there must be *some* married cowboys. At least one or two."

"Impossible," said Soup.

From where he perched on the fence, Soup extended a bare foot to pick a daisy with two of his gritty toes.

"How come, Soup?"

"Well," he said, "it's like this. Cowboys are out riding the range in all kinds of weather. They get muddy, catch cold, and always smell like cows. Or a buffalo."

"So what?"

Soup stared at me in disbelief. "Rob, when's the last time you helped yourself to a healthy whiff of Norma Jean Bissell?"

"Today," I said.

Soup had a point, though. Norma Jean smelled like a mixture of sugar and soap. To kiss her sweet cheek would be, I imagined, a lot like eating flowers. Or maybe even peppermint candy.

A dainty girl like Norma Jean Bissell, I was thinking, sure wouldn't ever be able to fall in love with a buffalo. Or with a boy who smelled like one. Tonight, I promised myself, I'd wash. Maybe even with a bar of soap; instead of doing what I usual did, which was sort of dust off my dirt with a towel. I really never took note I did this until Mama and Aunt Carrie started to point it out.

"Yup," said Soup, using his foot to fetch the daisy up into his fingers, "that there is the straight of it. You have to decide which."

"Which what?"

Soup took a breath. "Which you're intending to be someday. A cowboy, like me and Hoot Holler, or Norma Jean Bissell's poor old no-fun husband."

"Well," I said, "I sure don't guess I have to decide today."

"S'pose not." Soup flicked me the daisy. "Here," he said, "you can yank off the petals, one by each, and see if Norma Jean Bissell loves *you* or *perfume.*"

I twirled the daisy in my fingers. "I don't have to. Because I've already decided that today I'm going to be a cowboy. And maybe even forever."

As I said it, I didn't really swallow it all, because I was thinking about how the daisy, all yellow and white and soft, reminded me of Norma Jean's dress. Not that I wanted to wear a dress, or anything as dumb as that; yet I had to admit that Norma Jean was a whole lot better to look at than a cow.

Or even a horse like Thunderbolt.

"Rob, maybe on the way home, we ought to stop by the place where we hid our saddle."

"Check," I said. "And maybe we ought to start thinking about returning it. But how we'll ever haul it up through that high window sure beats me."

"Later," said Soup, jumping down off the fence. "I got a hunch, old top, that the saddle we borrowed last Saturday just might come in handy."

"Maybe," I said.

The place we'd hid the saddle was in a toolshed, behind Ferguson's Ice House. There was a pile of sawdust there; so Soup and I had dug a hole, planted the big cowboy saddle, and covered it up right snug.

We checked to see if it was still there. It was. So we re-covered the saddle and left it behind in the sawdust.

"Okay," said Soup. "What say, on the way home, we just sort of cut by Mr. Carlotta's place and say howdy to Thunderbolt?"

"Good idea," I told Soup.

As we arrived, Mr. Carlotta was there too. I noticed that he saw us coming, yet he didn't seem to eye us with mistrust. He even smiled.

"Howdy there, boys."

We smiled too. "Howdy, Mr. Carlotta."

He winked. "Have you two rascals been doing any horsebacking since I saw you last?"

Soup and I quickly shook our heads. "No, *sir,*" I added in a hurry.

"Good," he said. "You know, horses are a lot like ice. The kind of ice you skate on."

"How so?" Soup asked him.

Before answering, Mr. Carlotta whistled. Thunderbolt had not been in sight. Yet he must have known his owner's whistle, because he suddenly appeared, walking slowly out from behind a clump of sassafrass trees. He plodded up to the fence so Mr. Carlotta could stroke his black horse.

"It's like this," Mr. Carlotta told us. "You never skate on ice where you don't yet know its thickness. And, you shouldn't jump on a horse when you're strange to him. Saturday last, you lads were lucky that old Thunderbolt here was in a sleepy mood. And real docile."

Soup and I patted the big black horse.

"You mean," I asked, "that maybe Thunderbolt might've bucked the both of us off?"

Mr. Carlotta nodded. "This big studhorse has

made more than one jockey eat dirt."

Soup sort of shook his head. "Sure is hard to believe. Thunderbolt looks so doggone gentle."

The man patted the big black neck. "Oh, he's kitten enough, on water and oats. And on meadow grass too. This is spring. But come autumn, and he wanders off near to the orchard to nibble a few fallen apples, it fires him up like fury."

Soup looked blank. "Apples?"

"Honest. You see, ground apples tend to rot and partly ferment. You can't press tart cider from green apples. They have to be away over ripe."

"I like cider," I said.

Mr. Carlotta grinned. "I'd guess most folks do. But sweet cider's one thing. Cider that's turned has a lot more kick."

Soup said, "Then it's applejack."

"Right. I'd hate to think what would happen if old Thunderbolt drank some jack instead of brook water. He'd gallop through his meadow faster than an express train."

"Honest?" I asked.

Mr. Carlotta nodded. "In fact, a few years ago, I used to let Thunderbolt drink a few sips of applejack before a race."

"Would it make him win?" asked Soup.

"It sure made him run."

5

"Mama, where's the soap?"

I thought I heard my mother sigh. "Robert, have you tried looking in the soap dish?"

Sure enough, there was a bar of soap, smack dab under my nose. "Okay, I guess I got it located."

"Thank the goodness," said Mama. "By the way, before you begin, just exactly what are you planning to wash? If it's the cat . . ."

"No, it's *me*."

From the parlor where they were sitting, doing

some mending, I could hear Mama and Aunt Carrie chuckle. It was almost as if they couldn't swallow the fact that I intended to wash the Vermont off my face without being wrestled into the tub. Or held under.

I stood alone at the kitchen sink.

Chores and supper were over and I felt really chipper. I usual did on Friday nights. Soup and I always spent these special evenings together; at his house, or mine. But not tonight. If Soup wasn't already here, which he wasn't, it could mean only one thing. He probable got home late for chores and his folks sent him to bed with the chickens. Meaning *early*.

"Okay," I told the soap, "do your stuff."

Our bar of kitchen soap looked to be a brown glop of goo, lying in its dish, wading in a puddle of its own slime.

"Where's the rag, Mama?"

I heard her voice echo back from the parlor. "Look under the sink. And try not to mix the dirty rags in with the clean."

"I won't."

Peeling off my shirt, I wet a rag, soaped it proper, and then attacked my chest, arms, and neck with a sudsy scrubbing. The rag felt rough.

Yet maybe what I was feeling was mostly my own grit. There was a purpose in what I was doing. So secret was my plan that I didn't even want to allow my brain to study it much.

My target was Norma Jean Bissell.

"There," I said, smearing suds all over myself in every nook above my belt. "that ought to scrub me proper. Now to rinse off."

Soap stung my eye and I whispered a word that could have used some soaping itself. I wasn't quite sure exactly what the word meant; but Eddy Tacker, a mean kid in our class, used it whenever he fumed up angry. Or dropped a fly ball.

Janice used it too.

Maybe, I was thinking, I shouldn't use that word at all. Not even to myself. Because I sure didn't want to be like Eddy or Janice Riker. Eddy was a gorilla, while Janice was a gorilla disguised as a girl.

"Girls," Soup had once warned me, "are nothing but trouble."

Remembering the saddle we'd borrowed, and the horse we'd tried to ride, I then decided that maybe Soup was also trouble aplenty.

As I was just about to put my shirt back on, I took a closer squint at it. Then smelled it. My shirt bore a very familiar odor. Cow. I guess farmers, like Papa and me, didn't smell much more flowery than cowboys.

So I tossed my shirt into Mama's laundry basket and it wasn't even Saturday night. It was only Friday.

I fished out a clean shirt, the one that Mama always ordered me to save for Sunday morning and church. Looking into the hall mirror, I saw the upper half of a spotless boy. But my hair didn't look too gussy. Soup once said that my hair reminded him of mad straw. To me, my hair appeared to be a mix of dirt and electricity.

"I can fix it," I said. "I hope."

Hurrying out to the pump, I primed it from the bucket, jacked the handle and almost froze to death. But at least I could now, back at the mirror, plaster down my hair, using Aunt Carrie's hairbrush. That, I was thinking, was really only fair. She'd used that brush aplenty on me. Farther south.

"So long," I yelled to my folks.

"Where are you going?" asked Mama, who couldn't see me or wonder why I was now looking so spiffy.

"Oh, just out for a walk," I storied.

Well, it was sort of true, I thought; even if I didn't quite spell out where I was headed. Tonight, I thought with a grin, would be my very first *date*.

I cut across our back pasture, up the hill; then over the wire fence and through Mrs. Agnew's garden. Sneaking behind Frank Rooker's garage and along a hedge got me to my goal. And suddenly, there it was.

Norma Jean Bissell's.

The lights were on inside. Several yellow windows seemed to be almost pasted against the shadows of white clapboard. *Her house!* Those two words rang out in my heart like little silver bells.

Or was it, instead, a warning gong?

If I leaped up the front stairs and rang the doorbell, would this thoughtless act of folly seal my doom or end my possible career as a cowboy? I stared at the first step of the Bissell's porch, wondering if this was *my* first faulty step, or misstep, toward falling into the dreaded trap of husbandry.

Then I saw her!

Seeing a very pretty Norma Jean Bissell through the window made me forget about being a cowboy. Against my will, my brain hailed a farewell to dreams of horses, saddles, and spurs. "So long, Hoot!" my heart was hollering.

At that moment I would have agreed to become a dentist, an undertaker or even a *husband*.

"That does it," I said.

All I have to do now, I thought, is march right up to her front door, jingle the bell, and be invited in to spend an evening with Norma Jean Bissell, with memories that age could not wither.

Trouble was, my feet wouldn't budge.

Walking around in the shadows, after I finally got moving, started to loosen me up a mite. There was, I was thinking, no reason to be jittery. After all, I had sat in school with Norma Jean for years. So it certainly followed that I'd be able to sit in her parlor, cleverly slip my sneaky arm around her, look longingly into her eyes . . . and let her smell my soap.

"Wow!" I said.

There was precious little time to lose. Here I was and there stood the Bissell house. Yet it looked like a castle, a forbidden fortress; ready to be invaded by only the bravest of knights.

What, I asked, would Ivanhoe do?

As I dared a few steps closer to her front walk, I was thinking that it sure was a sorrow that Mr. Ivanhoe didn't live here in Learning, so he could mumble a few courageous words of advice. Maybe it was easy to face dragons, and dungeons, rather than *girls*.

I turned around again.

I'd have to plan my attack. Zero in on my target. Pinpoint my enemy. What was a *girl* anyhow? A girl, I then decided, was nothing more than a soft boy. Or a clean one. Up at Soup's house, I'd just knock on the door and *in* I'd parade. Bolder than brass.

"So," I decided, "that's what I'll do."

I ran up the stairs, crossed the porch in one mighty bound, and now . . . saw the tip of my finger only one inch from the button of Norma Jean Bissell's doorbell.

"Here I go," I whispered. "Charge!"

Heaven was only an inch away. My finger touched the button, yet I didn't really push. Golly, who'd answer the door? Maybe it might be *Mr.* Bissell.

"Git! Keep away from my innocent daughter," I was now imagining his voice to yell, "or I'll set the dog loose on you!"

No, I hoped, it would be *Mrs.* Bissell, who played the organ in church; and before that, she'd taught me in Sunday school. She'd probable smile at me; and she'd be holding a plate of fresh-baked cookies, or maybe I'd smell an inviting hint of a cherry pie wafting out from her oven.

Or would it be Norma Jean herself?

"Well," she might say, "what do *you* want, cowboy?"

"Smell me," I'd tell her. "Notice anything different?"

I pictured Norma Jean Bissell's face, suddenly closing her eyes, to inhale. Her frown would soften to the smile of an angel as her eager nose rewarded her with one more sugary sniff of my cleanliness.

"Soap," she would whisper.

"More pie, Robert?" Mrs. Bissell would offer, slapping one more giant slab onto my plate.

"Shucks, boy," Mr. Bissell would then say, "we folks don't even *own* a dog."

Soul aflame, my finger pushed the bell.

It rang!

The sound of that doorbell fired me into action. Escape! Leaping over the railing, I crashed through the shrubbery, running full tilt. Would old man Bissell take after me, I asked, with a shotgun? People, I knew, who rang doorbells and then ran were rarely popular. And maybe the Bissells *did* have a dog. His name was Fang and he was eight feet long with seven rows of razor-sharp teeth. Plus a pair of tusks like a boar hog.

I ran every step of the way home and near to collapsed as I gained the safety of our own kitchen door.

"Dating," I wheezed, "sure is exciting."

6

Saturday came.

So did Soup. He even came for a second breakfast, announcing to all us Pecks that he was extra hungry because of all he planned to do.

Aunt Carrie looked at Soup with a practiced and suspicious eye. There were few folks in the world, I'd noted, that couldn't be charmed by Soup's grin. Among those few, Aunt Carrie led the pack.

"Just what," she asked my pal, "are you planning?"

"Oh," said Soup, "just some stuff."

Earlier, when I saw Soup coming down the road, headed for our house, I'd noticed that he'd been toting a brown sack. Yet, as he arrived, he had been empty-handed.

As we finished our breakfast and bolted out of the door into the sunny freedom that only a Saturday morning can promise, I asked Soup about his burden.

"Okay," I said, "what's in the sack?"

"Don't tell," Soup warned me. "You'll see."

As we trotted around the corner of our barn, I followed Soup to the corn crib, under which he'd hidden his brown sack. He looked around with caution to be certain the two of us were unobserved. Opening the neck of the sack, Soup pulled out a tin bucket; from inside the bucket, he then lifted out a gallon jug filled with a liquid that was a pale amber.

"What is it, Soup?"

He grinned. "Cider."

But by the way he said the word, I had me a hunch that he wasn't quite letting loose of the truth. I'd seen cider before. Lots of times. What I was now seeing somehow looked a mite different. Much lighter in color.

"Soup," I said, "there's something about this cider that you know and I don't."

Soup hooked a finger through the ring of the jug and held it high. "You're right, Rob, old top. It's *applejack.*"

"Honest?"

"Yup."

"You're not planning for us to drink a whole bucket's worth of that dynamite, are you?"

"Nope. No way."

I sort of felt relieved. Sweet cider, especially around Halloween, was one thing. Applejack, I knew, was quite another.

"Where'd ya find it?"

Soup leaned against a corner of the corn crib, still holding his jug of jack. "I hooked it. Last fall, Pa pressed about ten kegs of sweet cider. We drank up most of it by Christmas, but not all. When winter comes, according to what I heard my folks say, you can let a barrel freeze up. Then you draw off what don't freeze."

"And that's applejack."

Soup nodded. "Let's get started."

"Where are we going?"

"You'll see." Soup winked at me.

Somehow, I knew. In my mind I could see myself

up on Thunderbolt's back, with Soup down on the ground, watching, as the horse drank his fill.

"Here," said Soup. "you carry the jug for a spell."

So I carried it as we cut due east, taking the shortcut in the direction of Mr. Carlotta's place. I was so excited, thinking how fast Thunderbolt would gallop, that I near dropped the jug.

"How about the saddle?" I asked.

"Maybe," said Soup, "we'll just sort of make matters a mite more simple and do without it. Because that's probable what real cowboys do whenever they're in a kind of rush to get stuff going."

Without asking, I knew the stuff Soup intended to get going. Thunderbolt and *me.*

"Perhaps," I said, "we ought to think this over before we hurry into it all." I knew it would be Soup's next move to hold the bucket while *I'd* have to hold back Thunderbolt.

Soup stopped. "You're too scared?"

I laughed at him, pretending how silly he was to think that I'd be afraid to ride a drunken racehorse at a hundred miles an hour. The thought, however, made me sweat.

We climbed over Mrs. Filmore's fence, waded through the brook on stones, and continued on our way. Only one or two more houses to pass by and we'd be coming up on Thunderbolt's meadow. One of the houses was a small white cottage. Out front, a tiny black Hoover automobile was parked.

"That car sure looks tired," I said.

Soup snorted. "It's got a right to. You know who lives here, don't you?"

"No," I told Soup. "Who does?"

"Miss Boland."

I stopped. "You mean Miss Boland our *nurse?*"

"Right."

A sudden idea was forming in my mind. Maybe, if we were planning to serve applejack to Thunderbolt and then, like a pair of fools, jump aboard . . . maybe a *nurse* would be just what we'd have need of. And fast.

"Soup, let's stop by and say hello."

He sighed. "I knew you'd want to postpone our ride."

"No," I said, "it's not that. It's just because Miss Boland's always so doggone good to all us kids and she sure is a pal to Miss Kelly."

My remarks, I had a hunch, would settle into Soup. I knew how he felt about Miss Kelly. Because when a kid like Eddy, or Janice, ever planned to do Miss Kelly dirt, Soup usual found a way to shortstop the deal. He never talked about it much. Yet I knew he respected Miss Kelly the same way I did.

"Okay," said Soup. "But just for a minute."

We hid our bucket and jug of applejack under Miss Boland's front stoop and knocked on her door. Then waited a long wait.

"It's probable too early," Soup said, "or she's decided to sleep late."

"Well," I said, "I don't guess we ought to rouse her."

With a shrug, Soup started to walk off the porch, and I was ready to follow. But then the door opened, causing us to turn around; and there she was.

"Morning, boys."

"Oh . . . howdy, Miss Boland."

"You fellas need something?"

As she asked the question, there seemed to be a tone in Miss Boland's voice that wasn't usual there. To me, she sounded sad. I took a step or two toward where Miss Boland's big body just about filled up her open door.

Soup must have sensed it too. His face, that had earlier been smiling, now wore a slight frown of concern.

"What's the matter, Miss Boland?" asked Soup.

In her hand was a letter. "This," she said, holding it up for us to see.

"Is it bad news?" I asked her.

Miss Boland sighed. "The worst."

"Did somebody die or something?" Soup asked.

"No, but I sure wish *I* could. This letter's from Montpelier, from the State Board of Education. Seems like our famous lady friend, Agatha Jones, can't come here to speak for Wednesday. But that's not the worst part. They're sending us someone *else.*"

"Who?" asked Soup.

Miss Boland scowled. "Dr. Elsa Pinkerton Uppit."

Soup and I just stared. I don't guess that I'd ever heard of Dr. Uppit and it appeared that Soup hadn't either. He shrugged.

"Come on inside, boys. Maybe the two of you will join me in a cool glass of lemonade while I explain. Right now, I need company."

The three of us trooped inside.

Excusing herself, Miss Boland waddled into her kitchen, returning a minute later with lemonade, cookies, and three glasses. As Soup and I gulped ours, Miss Boland fished a leaflet from her desk.

"Here's her photograph," she said. "In color."

Dr. Elsa Pinkerton Uppit looked to be an extremely large woman, with flaming red hair and a very unpleasant face.

"She looks mean," I said.

Miss Boland sighed. "She's even more ornery than she looks, boys. Five years ago, Dr. Uppit came here to Learning, took one glance at the little school you boys go to, and announced that it ought to be torn down."

Soup grinned. "We'd have no school."

Miss Boland grunted. "And there's something else you boys would never have again if this woman gets her way. You'd no longer have Miss Kelly for a teacher."

"No!" I said. Soup said it too.

"That's right, boys. Our new speaker on Miss Kelly Day is the sworn enemy of all of Vermont's one-room schools. She thinks teachers all ought to be young, so she's also out to get Miss Kelly fired."

"She can't do that," said Soup. "Can she?"

Our county nurse swigged a gulp of lemonade before answering. "Yes, she can. Dr. Uppit is the governor's cousin. Nobody in all of Vermont has more power in the field of education."

"And she's coming *here?*" Soup asked.

Miss Boland nodded. Her eyes looked a bit red and puffy, which sort of led me to believe that she'd been crying. I knew how much she and Miss Kelly liked each other. They were pals like Soup and me.

"We've got to *do* something," said Soup.

"Right," I said.

Our nurse shook her head. "Impossible. I hate to admit it, but Elsa Pinkerton Uppit is *not* coming to town to honor Miss Kelly. I bet she's coming to kick her out."

"No," said Soup. "We can't let her do it. Miss Kelly's the best teacher in the whole entire world."

"And she's going to get fired," I said, "if we let 'em tear down her little school."

That was when I saw a special expression on Soup's face. His frown slowly converted to a grin of mischief, a smile I knew only too well. His brain was now bubbling.

"It just might work," said Soup.

7

Soup told us his plan.

As he talked, Miss Boland's eyes grew wider and wider. Her mouth even popped open in total surprise. Finally his explanation eased to a halt.

"Wow," I breathed.

But then Miss Boland said, "I don't think that the three of us would ever be able to do it."

"Pardon me for saying this, Miss Boland," said Soup, "but ... shame on you for thinking we're licked before we even start. *You're* the one who said we could form a band or put on a show. You always say that folks can do whatever they got gumption enough to pull off."

Miss Boland looked amazed. "Me?"

"Yes'm," said Soup. "You."

"Well, I'll admit that I get a mite lathery whenever the rest of the town claims we *can't* do something."

"Right," said Soup. "So if you don't cotton to *my* plan, then somebody's got to whip up a better one. And jolly quick."

Miss Boland scratched her head. "It's risky. The

three of us could land ourselves into one heck of a heap of trouble."

I smiled. "Trouble's no stranger to Soup and me," I told Miss Boland.

"No, I imagine not. Kids like the pair of you *always* smell out trouble and jump right into it. Head first. But I'm a grown-up lady. Too old to get my hoofs all tangled in such a harebrained scheme."

"Maybe," said Soup. Getting up from the rocking chair, he paced to and fro in Miss Boland's parlor. "But let's not forget that maybe Miss Kelly's too old to ever land another job as a teacher in some other school. She's real *old.*"

"*Old?*" It was Miss Boland's turn to jump up to her feet. "I'll have you two turnips know that Miss Kelly's no older that *I* am."

Pausing, she looked at herself in the mirror. Her face darkened with defeat. "You're right," she finally said. "I'm fast fading. But I've still got *my* job. That's not all, boys." Miss Boland whacked her hand on the mantel shelf. "I've still got my backbone."

"Does that mean you'll *do* it?" asked Soup.

Miss Boland doubled her fists. "I'll do it."

Soup smiled. "I sort of figured you would. Because *your* part in this prank is the most fun. And the most important."

I saw Miss Boland shake her head. "Let's not stand around here and bicker about who's important. For now, it's Miss Kelly who's important, so best we all get cracking."

"What'll we do first?" I asked.

Tilting her glass, Miss Boland chugalugged the last drop of her lemonade. The ice tinkled the glass. "First," she said, "I'd suggest that you boys hasten down to Wilson's Hardware Store and ask Ben Wilson if he'll *donate* the paint."

"Okay," said Soup.

"And tell Ben that it's for Wednesday. Remind him, if he looks forgetful, that it's Miss Kelly Day. We'll need two gallons of pink paint and a tiny tube of green. Make it the sickest shade of green you can spy."

Soup nodded.

"Meanwhile," said Miss Boland, almost jumping up and down with enthusiasm, "I'll fetch myself over to Doc Witherspoon's and check up on a few symptoms. Just to make certain we're on the right track."

"We'll need some paintbrushes, too," said Soup.

"Maybe not. I can probable rustle up at least one from back yonder in the shed. I'll leave the brush out front and in plain sight."

"Check," I said. "One paintbrush."

"Perhaps," said Miss Boland, "we ought to jot down a list of the things we'll need. On the way over to Doc's place, I'll whoa in at Angelino's Beauty Parlor and get a you-know-what for my head."

Soup and I winked at each other. We knew what Miss Boland was fixing to borrow. And inside, I could hardly wait to see it.

"You boys had best hasten to the hardware store and then hustle straight back here. Soon as you return, start yourselves working on my car. You saw the leaflet on Dr. Elsa Pinkerton Uppit, in *color,* so you know what needs doing."

"Yes'm," said Soup.

"We sure do," I added.

"Then let's get ourselves in gear, boys, because there's not a second to waste or squander."

As we were leaving her house, Soup paused. "Thanks a whole lot, Miss Boland. You sure are one heck of a good sport."

Miss Boland smiled. "That's me."

Soup and I legged it for town, got there, and then ran smack dab into a major problem. There, sitting at the front door of the hardware store, was our first obstacle.

"Oh, *no,*" said Soup. "It's Janice Riker."

"Soup, we can't let *her* catch us. Not *now.*"

"We sure can't. Maybe," said Soup, "we can sneak around and duck in the back door."

"Good idea," I said. "There's only one soft spot. Wilson's Hardware Store doesn't *have* a back door."

Soup grinned. "I got it."

I took a cautious step backward. "If old Janice is what we're going to get, I don't want any part of it. Or her."

"Don't worry," Soup told me.

Usually, I'm not the worrying type. Yet whenever Luther Wesley Vinson tells me "don't worry," especially when Janice Riker and her fists are nearby, worry seems tough to duck.

"Hey, Janice!" Soup now yelled.

"Yeah?"

"Wanna see my new car?"

Janice stood up, planted both fists to her beefy hips, and snarled. *"You* ain't got no car."

"No? Well, as soon as Rob and I pick up some stuff at the hardware store, we'll show ya."

Janice Riker scowled. *"Show* me."

"Okay."

"Or *else.*" She cocked a fist the size of a bowling ball.

In we scooted, right past Janice Riker and all her

muscles, made our deal with Mr. Wilson, picked up two gallons of pink paint plus a tube of green, and marched out. I held my breath the entire time.

Janice was waiting.

"You guys don't own no car."

Soup scratched his head. "Tell ya what, Janice. If I don't own this car, you can do something really rotten. And I'll swallow all the blame."

"If you're lying . . ."

"Would I lie?" Soup asked.

"Yeah," said Janice Riker.

"Come on, Janice," said Soup. "It's this way if you're hankering to see my new car."

Janice shook a fist that sported at least forty-three knuckles. "This'd better not be one of your usual fancy tricks."

Soup and I headed toward Miss Boland's house, carrying the paint. Janice followed us. As we walked, he leaned over close to my ear to whisper. "Rob, we've got to drum up a way to get Janice really *mad.*"

I stared at Soup. "Mad? Are you kidding? Janice Riker was *born* mad. She's so sour she's probable half pickle and half barbed wire."

"Think," ordered Soup.

"Okay," I said to him, "I think you're crazy."

"Run," said Soup. "Janice won't be able to

catch us and that'll get her really steamed."

We ran.

Janice chased us. She was chasing me a lot closer because Soup was carrying only a tiny tube of green paint, while I was lugging two heavy gallons of pink. Good old Soup had done it to me again.

Somehow, with Soup way ahead of me and Janice close behind, I ran all the way to Miss Boland's house. Her black car was there, thank goodness, with a paintbrush lying on its hood. Yet I still didn't at all understand what Soup was up to.

I sure knew what Janice was up to. She was an inch behind me and gaining. My two gallons of pink paint now weighed a ton and that was gaining, too. A pound every yard I ran.

But as Janice caught me, Soup saved my life.

"Janice," he said, leaning on the fender of Miss Boland's black Hoover, "here's my car."

"You're a liar," puffed Janice. "This here car is Miss Boland's and everybody in town knows it. So now I get to do something mean."

"You win, Janice," said Soup. "You outsmarted me again. But whatever you do, please don't paint this car *pink,* because I'm washing it for Miss Boland and she'll half kill me."

While Janice painted the car pink, Soup and I rested in the shade, pretending to cry.

8

I couldn't sleep.

But I sure was dreaming. Each time my eyes would close, I'd envision Janice chasing me or painting me pink. Either that, or I'd remember Soup's bucket and his jug of applejack that was still stowed under Miss Boland's porch.

Wow! I sure got myself into one heck of a mess. That, plus the borrowed saddle.

Worst of all, Soup had involved good old Miss Boland into his plan. And now, hidden in her garage where no one would discover it, was her car . . . fresh painted, thanks to Janice.

Rolling over, I punched my pillow. "Darn it," I complained to the dark. "Why can't I sleep?"

Maybe, I was thinking, I'd be able to sleep in jail. There could be no doubt that prison was where Soup and I were destined to end up. And poor Miss Boland would be in the next cell.

"No," I sighed.

I didn't imagine that *anything* could turn out any worse than my *date* with Norma Jean Bissell, the night that I'd gotten as far as her doorbell.

Yet, I mused, things had thickened.

Tomorrow would be Wednesday. Our mayor had officially declared it a holiday for the whole town, no school, and my probable first day as a dangerous criminal.

Closing my eyes tighter than a miser's vise, I was determined to bag some rest. All I could see now was Thunderbolt. And then Janice Riker, madder than ever when she had finally learned how Soup and I had tricked her into painting Miss Boland's car pink.

Perhaps what bothered me the most was the fact that tomorrow would be Miss Kelly Day which I didn't want anyone, including all of us, to spoil. The one lady who was probable out to sour the festivities was no other than Dr. Elsa Pinkerton Uppit.

Tink!

Had I heard a noise? The answer had to be yes because I heard the mysterious sound twice more. On the glass of my window.

Tink! Tink!

Sitting up in bed, I got out quickly and leaped to the window. Someone was out there tinkling and I surely knew who.

It was Soup.

"Come on," he whispered up to me.

"Why? It's the middle of the night."

"Don't argue about it, Rob. You want tomorrow to turn out to be a proper day for Miss Kelly, don't you?"

"Sure I do."

"Then get yourself down here. Pronto."

Why I went I'll never know. Yet there was an urgent tone in Soup's voice that made me believe I'd best go or tomorrow would pan out even worse.

With a quickness of a hungry cougar, I crept out the window and along the roof and slid down our apple tree. As I hit Vermont, I noticed that Soup was toting a strange-looking box. Oddly enough, it looked like the gift his Uncle Clyde had mailed to him for his birthday.

"What's that?" I asked Soup.

"Hush," he whispered, "or you'll wake up your

Aunt Carrie and then we'll both catch it."

Soup was right, as usual. Aunt Carrie was indeed a light sleeper and had, in the past, claimed to have heard a bug sneeze. She was also, I knew, the type of person who would sound the alarm to every sleeping soul in the county if she suspected that Soup and I were up to midnight mischief.

"Let's go," Soup told me in a whisper.

"Where are we bound for?"

"You'll see."

Soup was wrong. The sky was cloudy with no moon; I could barely see Soup.

We walked along the dirt road, uphill, headed away from town. Soup let me carry the box which was, to me, still a mystery. My pal seemed to be in one hustle of a hurry so I had to trot to keep up, even though the gravel stung my bare feet. As we passed the place where our dirt road ended, meeting the paved county road, Soup stopped.

"This is it," he said.

"It's *what?*" As I spoke, I hitched up the bottoms of my yellow polka-dot pajamas.

"Rob, old top, you'll soon savvy."

Opening his box, Soup removed several articles: a stack of white cardboard rectangles, three metal plates that had letters cut into them, and a bottle.

"What's in the bottle, Soup?"

"Ink."

"We're not going to *write* out here, are we?"

"No, we're going to print."

As he held up his three plates, I saw that the letters spelled X-O-P. The word sure was an odd one. No odder, I was thinking, than Luther Wesley Vinson, known as the mad midnight printer.

"Soup, I hate asking a stupid question, but I gotta know. What in heck is a *xop?*"

"It isn't anything," said Soup.

Kneeling down, Soup laid one of his blank cardboards flat on the road and twisted open his bottle of ink.

"Remember what Miss Boland told us," Soup said. "Well, here's where we'll tack up our signs. Get it?"

"No. All I'm getting is tired. I don't guess I really want to print anything. Not even XOP. All I want to do is crawl back home and into my bed."

"Hand me the dabber," said Soup.

"The what?"

"It's in the box. You know, it's what we use to dab the ink over the letters."

I handed Soup the dabber. Taking it, he inked it; then rolled the ink along his three letters. He's nuts, I was thinking. Who else would venture out here at midnight and print XOP on a sign?

"There," he said, "that does it."

"Does what?"

Soup held up his work.

POX, I read.

"Got it?" he asked me. "Now you know why we're doing this. For the same reason we went to the hardware store and got the little tube of green paint."

Even during the daytime I don't think too well. But at night, I'm a first-class dope. Why, I asked myself, was I here, standing uproad in the dark, reading POX, and in my bare feet?

"Okay," said Soup. "Get 'em up."

I asked him what he meant.

"As I print the signs, start tacking them on trees or fenceposts along the road, and we'll work our way home. Look in the box and you'll find a tack hammer and a box of tacks."

Too tired to quibble, I said, "Okay."

Soup printed POX. I tacked. We did it about every twenty feet, working our darkening way downroad, toward home. At least, I told myself as the hammer missed the tack and whacked my thumb, I was getting closer and closer to my bed.

"We're done," Soup wearily announced. "Rob, this here is the very last of our signs."

I tacked up the last POX to a roadside elm.

Soup sighed. "I sure hope we've got our geography straight. I'd hate to imagine that we nailed up all of our signs on the wrong road."

As I stood there in my pajamas, rubbing my drooping eyes, I sort of began to realize what Soup was up to. Bits and scraps of his crazy plan swirled around in my sleepy brain.

"Let's go home, Soup. I'm beat."

"Best we do, or we'll never get up for chores come morning. I sure wish Pa had cows that took Wednesday off."

"So long," I told Soup when at last we had reached my house. "See ya tomorrow."

I watched him trudging up the hill toward home, toting his box, and whistling. Soup sure was an unusual kid. He was half brains and half trouble, yet no one would ever call Luther Wesley Vinson dull. Life with him, I thought, as I finally crept back into my bed, was sort of like living in a comic book.

Soup was adventure, peril, and fun.

Yawning, I closed my eyes and thought about only one word as I drifted off to sleep:

POX.

9

At ten o'clock on that Wednesday morning, both Soup and I arrived breathless at Miss Boland's house and knocked.

"Good morning, boys." As she opened the door, I couldn't quite believe what I saw. My hands rubbed my eyes. There stood Miss Boland in a bright flowered dress. On her head rested a flaming red wig.

"Well," she asked, "tell me the straight-out truth. Do I look enough like Dr. Elsa Pinkerton Uppit?"

Soup was speechless. So was I. The pair of us just stood on Miss Boland's front porch and stared at what used to be our county nurse. Soup finally found words to express his total awe.

"Holy red eye!"

Miss Boland sighed. "Perhaps I'm only fooling myself. But today, my trusty lads, I've got to fool a whole town."

"You'll do," I told her.

"Rob," she told me, "skip out to my mailbox, please, and see if the weekly's arrived. Luther, you fetch yourself around the back, like a willing lad, and open up my garage doors."

I brought her the weekly newspaper.

Miss Boland almost tore it out of my hands and opened it up; together we read the big bold headline:

MISS KELLY DAY, it said.

Soup returned, and the two of us listened inside the parlor as Miss Boland read aloud from the paper.

"Learning today is happy to celebrate. We honor Miss Winifred Kelly, who, for the past thirty years, has served our community, instilling in our youngsters both education and character."

Soup said, "That sounds nifty."

I watched Miss Boland's eyes scan a few paragraphs, then continue reading aloud. "Following the brass-band parade, in which Miss Kelly will ride in Mayor Doolittle's open car, and also featuring Hoot Holler, a picnic for all will be enjoyed on the village green."

I smiled. The thought of hot dogs, soda, and ice cream almost nudged me enough to wish away the morning.

"And," read Miss Boland, "the highlight of the day will be marked by the arrival of Dr. Elsa Pinkerton Uppit, who hails from Montpelier, and comes here to Learning to honor us with a speech. Her subject is New Horizons in Vermont Education."

Miss Boland frowned and snorted.

"Well," she said, "the three of us have a few *new horizons* for Dr. Uppit, don't we, boys?"

"We sure do," said Soup.

Our nurse read more. "Dr. Uppit arrives today in her well-known pink Hoover motorcar, and all residents of Learning are urged to welcome her, giving Dr. Uppit our most courteous attention."

I saw Miss Boland's chubby fist whack the newspaper. Her jaw was set into a determined expression, which led me to believe if *anybody* could stand up in front of a crowd and pretend to be Dr. Uppit, *she* could.

"Is your speech all written?" I asked her.

Miss Boland's face turned suddenly pale as she sunk her overstuffed body into an overstuffed chair.

"What's wrong?" Soup asked her.

Before answering, Miss Boland pulled the red

wig from her head. "Jeepers, I *knew* there was *some-thing* I forgot to prepare. My *speech*. Boys, I don't even have one foggy idea of what I'm going to say."

Soup paced back and forth. "Well, you certain can't just stand up there on the bandstand and wave your wig."

"No, I sure can't. But I've never made a speech before in my entire life. I'll keel over with stage fright. I can open my mouth, but no words'll flutter out."

"Quick," said Soup. "Where's some paper and a pencil?"

Miss Boland weakly pointed to a desk in the corner. "Help yourself."

Soup made a leap for the desk, grabbed a pencil, and started to write. But after scribbling down one word, he abruptly stopped.

"What have you got so far?" I asked Soup.

"Hello," he said.

"Well, that's a start," groaned Miss Boland.

Soup erased his word. Inspiration was, however, beginning to grace his face and the pencil now seemed to take on fresher purpose. The faster he wrote, the closer his nose sunk to the paper. Even more, he began to read aloud as he wrote his words.

"Citizens of Learning," said Soup. "It fills my

heart with gladness to look out yonder and see so many smiling faces. Small wonder. Because today, we meet here on this important occasion, to give a pat on the back to a lady who loves her kids."

"Hey," said Miss Boland. "That's not bad."

"Thanks," said Soup.

"Keep going."

"As you know," Soup said as he wrote, "Miss Kelly's been a teacher in this here town for thirty years. And she's loaded up lots of kids with a pile of smart education. Except for Janice."

Miss Boland looked surprised. "Janice?"

"You can cross out whatever you don't like," said Soup. "But please don't stop me now. I'm rolling hot."

"We won't," I told him.

Soup continued. "For example, Miss Kelly knows a lot of stuff about Mongolia and places like that. But I'm not here on this wonderful day to talk about Asia." Soup paused. "I'm here to talk about what a great school Miss Kelly teaches in and the super kids that have to sweat over all those tons of homework."

As he wrote, I was starting to understand what Soup was into. More trouble. The speech didn't sound as if it had been written by Dr. Uppit. It was all Dr. Vinson.

"And," said Soup, his pencil flying along every line, "maybe Miss Kelly does make her kids *wash* too much. But remember this. Being clean is healthy and keeping well is so important, because your dedicated county nurse, Miss Boland, would say likewise."

Miss Boland smiled. "That's catchy."

Pulling out another page of paper, Soup kept writing, sharing with us his words.

"What's more, Miss Kelly understands that even the best and smartest kids can stumble into trouble. But if they do, and their little hearts are in the right place, those same kids should *not* get punished."

I saw Miss Boland look at Soup with a wary eye. But she didn't say "boo." Maybe she was thinking that Soup's speech beat no speech at all.

"So it's my honor and pleasure," said Soup, "to have come all the way here from Montpelier, our state capital, to pay tribute to a teacher whose very name stands for *new horizons in education.*"

Miss Boland nodded. "Is that all?"

"Not quite," Soup answered her. "I just thought up some more. Here goes. . . . Even though the school Miss Kelly teaches in isn't very big, it will always stand plenty tall in the hearts of all you local folks who went there as kids."

"Good," I said.

The telephone rang. Miss Boland sprang up from her chair as if she'd been shot. She put the phone to her ear.

"Hello. Yes, this is Miss Boland. Oh, it's you, Clarence. What's up?" There was a pause, and then Miss Boland said, "Early?" Longer pause. "I see. Yes, I'll be there as soon as I can. Good-bye."

She hung up. Her face was ashy white. And once again she slumped into the chair, staring straight ahead.

"Boys, we're *sunk.*"

"What's the trouble?" asked Soup.

"The worst possible news. Clarence Goodnew's the chairman of our Board of Education. He just got a phone call from Dr. Uppit, who's already as far as Dixon Corners. That means she'll be here in Learning a half hour *early.*"

"*No,*" said Soup.

"Yes! And once she reaches town it'll be too late. Now there's no way we can put our plan into action. She'll be cruising down the county road in about fifteen minutes. You boys will never be able to get out there in time."

Soup grinned. "There's a shortcut."

10

"Hurry," said Soup.

Leaving poor Miss Boland behind to study her speech, put her wig back on her head, and then get to her pink car, Soup and I dashed from her house.

From under her porch, Soup pulled out the bucket and his jug of applejack. We legged it to the toolshed behind Ferguson's Ice House and reclaimed our borrowed cowboy saddle. Plus the blanket.

How we managed to drag everything all the way to Mr. Carlotta's pasture I will never know. We just did it.

Thunderbolt, luckily or unluckily for us, must have remembered the carrots. Seeing us, over he plodded. Reaching over the top rail of the fence, I gave the big black horse a friendly pat.

"He wants a carrot, Soup."

Soup grinned. "As I see it, old Thunderbolt is

about to get something with a lot more kick to it than a carrot. Okay, let's throw the saddle on his back. But before we do, you didn't forget to grab our tube of green paint, did you?"

"No," I said, patting my hip pocket, "I got it right in here, safe and sound."

"Good."

Soup and I cinched the saddle as tight as we could tug.

"Okay," said Soup, uncorking the jug and gurgling applejack into his pail, "mount up."

"Won't we need a bridle?'

Soup sighed. "It's tough to try to remember *everything*. Well, there's no time to search now. What we need is *speed*. And old Thunderbolt's got it."

I mounted while Thunderbolt drank.

"He sure likes it," said Soup. "Hang on."

"Aren't *you* coming, too?"

Soup smiled. "No sense in two of us going. When you get there, you know what to do with the green paint."

I started to get off. "Look," I told Soup, "the two of us are in this mess together, and we're *both* in it all the way. Unless you come I'm not going."

Soup sighed. "Okay, you win. But you ride in the front because I don't guess I want to look."

As he spoke, Thunderbolt slurped up the last drop and even licked the bucket. Soup climbed up into the saddle, grabbed my waist with both his arms and waited. We waited more. Thunderbolt just stood still. And then he did one more thing.

He burped.

"Applejack," said Soup.

One time, at a circus, I'd seen a daredevil shot out of a cannon. But it was nothing at all to the way Thunderbolt suddenly shot across the meadow. His first leap must have spanned a good twenty feet.

"*Ahhhhhhhhh*," screamed Soup.

But I didn't scream. I was too scared to even open my mouth. Thunderbolt increased his speed. Trees and bushes were whizzing by in a green blur.

"Whoa," I pleaded.

"Say it again," hollered Soup. "I don't think Thunderbolt heard you."

So I kept yelling "Whoa!" again and again, but Thunderbolt only galloped faster. The louder I yelled, the faster he sped. I closed my eyes.

"Oh, *no*," I heard Soup moan.

Opening my eyes quickly, I suddenly saw what lay dead ahead, directly in our path. It was a fence.

"Whoa!" I screamed.

I wondered if Thunderbolt would stop. But I

sure didn't have long to wonder. He didn't. Nor did he even bother to slow down. Up we went. All I can remember is leaving the saddle and performing some strange variety of back flip.

Three things happened.

Thunderbolt landed, Soup landed, and then so did I. The two of us were somehow still in the saddle, yet Soup was now in front and I was in back, holding on to him.

"Whoa!" cried Soup.

Cars, I knew, finally would run out of gas and stop. But when, I was silently asking myself, would old Thunderbolt run out of applejack? He sure got a lot of miles to the gallop. All I could hear was Soup's screaming and the thunder of Thunderbolt's hoofs.

Shutting my eyes, I prayed. If I ever get out of this mess alive, I promised, I would never again *look* at another horse. Or consider growing up to be a cowboy.

At the speed we were now riding, I feared that I wouldn't be growing up at all.

"He's slowing down," said Soup.

My pal was right. The green blurs of passing vegetation were appearing to be more and more in focus. Thunderbolt, thank the goodness, was at last running low on applejack.

When some horses get winded, or tired, they merely slow down. Thunderbolt just stopped. Planting his front hoofs, he pulled up short. Soup and I didn't stop at all. Instead, the two of us flew through the air; and I was hoping that somehow I'd suddenly sprout either wings or landing gear.

It was a good thing we didn't land on rocks. Looking on the bright side, *prickers* were far softer, more yielding. But not exactly what you'd honest call comfortable.

"Ouch," said Soup.

So did I. In fact, we said an *ouch* for each and every pricker that was tucked into us. We said it several dozen times. Thunderbolt looked at us, curled back his lip, showed his teeth in a wide horselaugh, and snorted *"Hic."*

"Come on," said Soup. "We don't have any more time to waste pulling out prickers. Because over there is the county road."

We did what needed doing.

Opening up our tiny tube of paint, I covered Soup's face with little green spots and then he put some green freckles on me.

"How do I look?" Soup asked.

"Real sick," I told him. "Like you're near to dying from some sort of POX."

"Good," said Soup. "Because here comes a little

pink car, and it sure does look like a Hoover."

Dashing out into the road, I saw a familiar sign. It was white, rectangular, and it read POX. For some odd reason, our plan was on the brink of working, yet I never really understood how.

Seeing the two of us in the road, the driver of the little pink Hoover slowed and halted. Behind the wheel was a confused-looking person. A very large lady with very red hair. Yet, in my mind, there was no doubt that she was our enemy, Dr. Elsa Pinkerton Uppit . . . the education woman who wanted to close our school and fire Miss Kelly.

As she cranked down her window to talk to us, Soup and I approached her car.

Just as we had practiced, we limped, coughed, choked, staggered, and even tried vainly to throw up. The expression on Dr. Uppit's face slowly turned from confusion to dread.

"We're *sick*," Soup told Dr. Uppit.

"Maybe even dying," I said.

I saw Dr. Uppit's eyes read one of our roadside signs. Then she looked back at us. "Don't come any closer," she warned.

"The pox is spreading through Learning," I heard Soup tell her. "People are screaming and keeling over in the streets. Can you take us away in your car?"

"But I don't understand," said Dr. Uppit. "I talked to Clarence Goodnew only a few mintues ago on the telephone. He never mentioned a *pox.*"

Soup looked sad. "I know. My name is Junior Goodnew. Just as Pa hung up the phone, his face broke out with green blotches, and he keeled over in pain."

Dr. Uppit's face almost froze into an expression of sheer horror. "What . . . what kind of pox is it?"

Soup coughed. "Mongolian," he wheezed.

I screamed, clutched my belly, fell to the ground, and rolled around in pretended agony.

"He's a goner," said Soup as I suddenly lay still on the road and twitched. "So maybe I best jump into your car, with you, and let you drive me to a hospital. Or to a cemetery."

"No!" screamed Dr. Uppit.

Her motor roared as her frantic shifting was grinding the gears. Never before had I ever seen a car, not even a Hoover, turn around so fast. In clouds of anxious dust, Dr. Uppit gunned her engine and headed away from Learning and the pox. So fast that I wondered if her tank contained not gasoline but applejack.

"We did it," said Soup.

11

"Let's go, Soup."

It took us several minutes to take down all our POX signs and hide them in a hole under a boulder.

Thunderbolt, who was now very calm, was waiting for us, standing under the old cowboy saddle as if expecting us to come over and help him nurse his hangover. His eyes looked to be a shade on the crimson side and his big black head was slightly drooping. Somehow, I suspected that he was faking.

We climbed into the saddle.

Our return trip took its own sweet time. So did Thunderbolt. Yet it certain was a pleasant ride, seeing as our big old horse merely walked all the way back to the very spot where our wild gallop had begun. Sure enough, there was the empty pail and the empty jug.

I was glad to note that Mr. Carlotta, the man who owned Thunderbolt, didn't seem to be around. Probable in town, I thought, attending all the festivities.

"I hope we don't miss the parade," said Soup.

"Golly," I said, "a real brass band. And then, on top of that, Hoot Holler. I don't guess we'll want to miss *him*."

We were about to loosen the cinch and pull our borrowed cowboy saddle off Thunderbolt's back.

"I got an idea, Soup."

"Like what?"

"Well, it'll sure save us time if we lead old Thunderbolt over to Mr. McGinley's barn. It'll make returning the saddle a lot easier."

Soup didn't look too receptive to my suggestion until I finally used the magic word.

"As I see it, Soup, it'll mean a lot less *work*."

"Rob, old top, you're really thinking."

So, with Thunderbolt's assistance, we easily toted the big cowboy saddle as far as the fence that separated Mr. Carlotta's meadow from Mr. McGinley's red barn. It was on our way toward town.

"This," said Soup, "is the easy part."

"The hard part," I said, "will be boosting that old saddle up to that window up yonder. It's hopeless, Soup. We'll never be able to do it."

As he dismounted, Soup frowned with his eyes and eyebrows, yet smiled. I could tell he was sinking into a deep thought. I dismounted, too.

"Maybe," he said, "we *don't* return the saddle."

"Huh?"

"Leastwise, not just yet. Rob, old top, there's one thing I always wanted to do. I bet ya can't guess what it is."

I sighed. "Go to jail."

"Well," said Soup, "not quite. The one thing I really hanker to do is . . . *ride a horse in a parade.*"

"No," I said.

Soup punched my shoulder but not hard. "Rob, where's your spirit of adventure? Any kid can *watch* a parade go marching by. But you and I can be *in* it."

"I won't do it, Soup. We're in enough trouble already. And maybe, in case you possible forgot, Miss Boland is still in it up to her chubby neck."

"Ah," said Soup, pacing to and fro along the fence, "that's part of my plan."

"It is?"

"Sure. When we're in the parade, maybe we can manage to attract more than a bit of attention and pull some of the heat off Miss Boland."

"Maybe."

"No maybe about it. Rob, riding Thunderbolt in the parade will actual be the biggest thing we can do all day for Miss Kelly."

"Okay," I said.

Why I agreed to Soup's madness I'll never truly know. Perhaps, deep inside, I still wanted to be a cowboy, instead of being a failure. Or a husband.

"Here we go," said Soup. "Mount up."

So there we were, once again, up in the saddle on Thunderbolt's back, headed for Learning and Miss Kelly Day. Soup rode in front. I rode behind, hanging on. Thunderbolt, thank goodness, was more docile than ever, walking so slowly that I could near count almost a full second between his *clips* and his *clops*.

However, we rode Thunderbolt all the way to the gate. Soup stayed up in the saddle while I skinned down to slip the bars. It gave me second thoughts.

"Soup, maybe riding Thunderbolt out of his pasture and into town isn't such a whopper of a good idea."

"Don't worry," he told me. "Besides, you want Norma Jean Bissell to see you in the parade, don't you?"

I did. Yet I was nagged by doubt as I climbed back into the saddle behind Soup. "Why can't we just go and watch the parade like anyone else?"

"Because," said Soup, *"anybody* can be anyone else. After all, we're Luther Vinson and Robert Peck, aren't we? So let's show the whole town we're not just anybody. We're *somebodies."*

We rode slowly into town.

I was starting to doubt what we were doing, more and more. Soup, I was deciding, was nuts. And I had to pick a lunatic for a pal.

"Maybe," I said hopefully, "we've missed the parade. It's probable already marched down Main Street."

Soup turned to look at me over his shoulder. "Not a chance. One thing I've learned about parades."

"What's that?"

"They never," said Soup, "begin on time."

Soup was right.

As old Thunderbolt turned the corner into town, I saw the brass band in their bright red uniforms. Mr. Delvin Furdock, our local constable, was trying to get everyone organized. Nobody was. There seemed to be an argument about whether our new red fire truck would go in front of the band or trail behind it.

"Rob, old top," said Soup, "we're just in time."

I sighed. "Great." Secretly, I was sort of hoping that we'd missed the parade and that we'd be able to sneak into town without too much notice.

No dice.

The band started to form into ranks. Their drum major blew a whistle and off they marched, coming our way.

"Good news," said Soup. "We're in front."

"In *front?*"

"Rob, you and I and old Thunderbolt are going to *lead* the parade up Main Street."

"No," I said. Yet it was true. Soup and I were now in front of the brass band.

Behind us, the band members lifted their instruments and broke into the loudest and brassiest blast of marching music that I'd ever heard. Soup and I both jumped. Yet our reaction was mild compared to Thunderbolt's. He bucked straight up in the air.

"Holy *applejack!*" Soup cried out.

It was the wrong word to say. I don't know who else heard it, but I sudden knew that Thunderbolt sure did. Apparently, for some strange reason, even the mention of *applejack* was enough to excite our horse.

Thunderbolt bolted!

If our gallop through Mr. Carlotta's pasture was fast, our current speed was a whole lot faster. All I could think to do was grab on to Soup and hang on.

"Yippeee!" yelled Soup.

Hearing such encouragement, Thunderbolt doubled his speed. Eyes closed, I prayed for a quick and painless death. I kept remembering how we had foolishly forgotten a bridle. We had no reins. Thunderbolt had a free head, to gallop wherever he chose; and at any speed that his fondest memories of a bucket of applejack would spur.

I'd heard, a year or so ago, that Janice Riker's daddy had been arrested, in town on a Saturday night, for drunken driving. It made me wonder how long the jail sentence would be for drunken galloping.

As we flew by a group of citizens, I heard somebody ask, "Is that Hoot Holler?"

"Whoa," pleaded Soup. The way he said it made me pry open my eyes and force myself to look over Soup's shoulder at what lay dead ahead.

It was the bandstand in the park.

Thunderbolt was heading for it at an impossible speed. His hoofs never seemed to be touching the turf. To make matters worse, the bandstand was not empty. Standing on it, all alone, was no other except Mr. Cyrus McGinley.

I saw Mr. McGinley growing larger and larger as Thunderbolt charged closer and closer. Mr. McGinley looked up at us.

"Help!" he said.

The bandstand stood up high, as if the person who had designed it wanted it to be a second story, not a first. It was sort of a little upstairs on stilts. And just as Thunderbolt reached it, going at least eighty miles an hour, he stopped. I heard our saddle cinch snap.

Soup and I were not so lucky. We didn't stop.

Still seated in the saddle, with no horse, the two of us sailed through the air, landed on the upper floor of the bandstand, and whizzed by Mr. Cyrus McGinley. I somehow knew that this was the end, my finish. Soup and I would surely perish.

We skidded off the other side of the platform, fell, and landed in a heap. I felt every bone and decided they were all broken. Soup, however, seemed to recover faster; and my insane pal was the first to speak to Mr. McGinley, who had apparently been lucky enough to dodge us.

"Hi," said Soup. "We found your saddle, Mr. McGinley, and we're returning it. But please, sir, don't offer us a reward."

Mr. Cyrus McGinley, I recalled, wasn't noted for a pleasant disposition or for liking kids who were troublesome or loud. Scowling, he looked down at us, then to Thunderbolt, who stood nearby, snorting. Mr. McGinley snorted too.

"Get that dangfool animal away from here. And fetch that worthless old saddle to the dump. It belonged to my wife's brother and I don't like either of 'em."

"Yes, *sir*," I told him.

I tried to sound extra polite as Mr. McGinley served on our local Board of Education. He, I figured, would stand soldily behind Miss Kelly. According to what Mama always said, a lot of changes had been proposed in the town of Learning, and Cyrus McGinley had voted against every precious one.

Soup actually helped me heft the old cowboy saddle up and onto Thunderbolt's back. Up on the bandstand, Mr. McGinley ventured a step closer, squinting at us over his halfmoon glasses.

"Say," he said, "there's something peculiar going on around here. Mighty peculiar."

"I smell trouble," Soup whispered.

12

Mr. McGinley's eyes narrowed with distrust.

"*What*," he asked us, "in the unholy name of tarnation is on your faces? Have you boys took sick with some crazy disease?"

It hit me! Soup and I had forgotten to scrub off our freckles of sickly green paint.

"Oh, *that*," Soup told him. "It's part of our costume for the parade. You know, for Miss Kelly Day."

Mr. McGinley grunted. "For a minute there, I was thinking that you two nuts were coming down sick with the pox." He squinted at us. "What are you two supposed to be dressed up as?"

"Oh," said Soup, "we're Mongolians."

"Okay, you boys best hightail out of here because I got to git the bandstand ready for Hoot Holler and Dr. Uppit. If I had time, I'd whale the tar out of both of you."

Soup and I didn't argue. We smiled, turned, and led Thunderbolt away.

Finding a spot of cool shade, behind Mr. Edgar Petty's barbershop, we tied Thunderbolt comfortably to a tree with an old hunk of rope. We then washed our faces partly clean in the men's room of Gil Cooper's gas station.

Then we strolled casually up Main Street.

The band was still playing. Looking around, I felt glad so many folks had come to town to honor Miss Kelly. Right then, I saw a lady jump up and down, and point. My eyes followed the line of her finger.

Sure enough, he was coming, riding on a white horse, holding his famous silver guitar, and very much a part of the long parade. Behind him rolled Learning's spanking new red fire truck. But I looked only at Hoot.

"Wow," said Soup. "Now there's what I'd call a real genuine cowboy."

"Yup," I said, stretching my neck up to see all I could, "he certain is."

Hoot Holler smiled, waved, and winked to the people who were lined up along Main Street. To look at a guy like Hoot almost made me forget all about Norma Jean Bissell. For at least a minute.

Trailing the fire engine came Mayor Doolittle's car. He owned the spiffiest wheels in town, the kind of automobile that could travel with its top up or down. Now it was down, the mayor was steering, and seated in the back was Miss Kelly. I hoped she wasn't worried about Dr. Uppit.

"Hooray!" yelled Soup. "Three cheers for Miss Kelly because she's our teacher."

I saw lots of folks clapping. The applause made Miss Kelly smile and wave.

But the parade was far from over. Girl Scouts paraded by. So did Boy Scouts and the Campfire kids. After those groups marched the American Legion, in blue uniforms, and the Veterans of Foreign Wars.

"Here she comes," somebody said.

That was when I saw a pink Hoover. Yet it wasn't Dr. Elsa Pinkerton Uppit's car. It was Miss Boland's. Our nurse, in her disguise, sat behind the wheel and looked as if she wanted to be somewhere else. She had pulled the red wig down over the upper half of her face as though she was doing her best to hide.

"Now," said Soup.

"Welcome to town, Dr. Uppit," the two of us hollered, just as we had earlier agreed to do. Turning to me, Soup said in his loudest voice, "See? She looks just like all her pictures."

Behind me, a gentleman passed a comment to his wife. "That," he said, "is near to about the sloppiest paint job I ever saw on a Hoover."

I laughed, remembering how Soup had tricked Janice into doing all the work with the paintbrush.

When the last of the parade, comprised of the high school drum and bugle corps, had marched by, Soup and I darted through the crowd and made a dash for the park. Things looked different now. Rows of folding chairs had been set up in front of the bandstand. Miss Kelly was seated in the very front row, exactly in the middle, the place of special honor. She was all alone.

Soup and I almost broke our necks racing over to grab the two seats on either side of her to keep her company.

"Well," said Miss Kelly, "I was wondering if I'd be seeing the two of you today. And here you both are. Thank you for coming."

The chairs all around us filled quickly. Up on the platform of the bandstand, Mayor Doolittle held up his hands for silence.

"Folks," he said, "as you all know, I'm not standing up here in front to make a speech."

Everyone applauded.

The mayor coughed. "The lady you all came to listen to is seated up here with me. So, without further ado, allow me to introduce a visitor who's arrived in town all the way from Montpelier. In her famous pink car. Let's hear a warm and hearty welcome for . . . Dr. Elsa Pinkerton Uppit."

Amid the applause, forward stepped Miss Boland in her flowered dress and a red wig. As she did so, I stole a quick sideways glance at Miss Kelly. Our teacher's slight frown melted into an expression of total surprise.

"*She's* not . . ." Miss Kelly started to say.

"Don't worry," Soup told her. "I heard tell there was a last-minute change in the program. Because of illness."

The applause behind us quieted and I heard Miss Boland clear her throat. The speech that Soup had hurriedly scribbled was now crackling, unfolded in her hands. The paper fluttered a mite. Miss Boland looked as if she wanted to either scream or run.

Miss Kelly's eyes grew wider. Her mouth slowly fell open in absolute shock. She *knew.*

"Oh, *no,*" Miss Kelly sighed.

"Yes," said Soup. "But please, Miss Kelly, don't give her away. We've got to pretend that she's the real Dr. Uppit."

Miss Kelly looked at me, then at Soup. "A last-minute change because of illness," she said. "I wonder what kind of illness it was."

"Mongolian pox," whispered Soup.

Stretching up a finger, Miss Kelly touched my face, noticing how her fingertip was now a sickly green. "Pox?" she asked me.

"Yes'm," I said. "In a way."

"If," she said, "I ever live through these next few minutes, without dying of laughter, I shall indeed be most grateful . . . to, shall we say, all *three* of the most loyal friends that anyone could ever deserve."

Miss Boland delivered Soup's speech, word for word; except for the part about Janice and too much homework. She even spiced up her address, here and there, with a few tributes of her own. Our nurse had lots of good stuff to say about how our town, and all its kids, ought to honor our teacher.

Even though I knew it was Miss Boland up there, and not Dr. Uppit, hearing it all sort of made me swallow.

Miss Kelly Day was turning up roses.

As soon as Miss Boland took a bow, people

clapped even louder. If there was anything, I thought, that folks enjoyed, it was the last and final word of a short speech. Especially prior to a picnic.

"And now," announced Mayor Doolittle, "it sure does give me great pleasure to introduce Vermont's most famous singing cowboy. Folks . . . here's Hoot Holler."

There he stood.

Hoot was tall, lanky, and wearing his most glittery duds. Spangles covered his shirt and cowboy hat, and his silver guitar sparkled brighter than a sun shower. Nobody seemed to even dare a breath. His gifted fingers began to strum lazy chords and then his voice cracked out his famous theme song, "Pajamas and Spurs."

> *"Oh . . . when . . . it's . . .*
>
> *Moonlight on the prairie,*
> *I unsaddle my ol' horse.*
> *Headin' to the bunkhouse, which is*
> *Right nearby, of course.*
>
> *My head done hits my pilla, and my*
> *Snores are near to purrs.*
> *Sleepin' cozy snug in my*
> *Pajamas and my spurs."*

Hoot wailed out all seventeen verses, through his talented nostrils; and it was all Soup and I could do just to hold back our whooping. I took note that even Miss Kelly tapped her shoe a few times to the beat of Hoot Holler's music.

After the show, everybody in town stampeded forward just to sneak a close-up look at Hoot or beg an autograph. He shook lots of friendly hands.

Miss Kelly, however, made her way forward; but not to fight the crowd around Hoot Holler. Instead, she briskly walked to the back of the bandstand to catch Miss Boland, who was making a hurried exit. Soup and I tagged along.

"Dr. Uppit?" asked Miss Kelly in her most pleasant voice.

"Hush," hissed Miss Boland. "If folks in this town see the two of us together, the jig is up."

Miss Kelly smiled and took her hand. "Dr. Uppit . . . please allow me to congratulate you on a most . . . moving speech." Her voice was a bit husky. "I'm a lucky woman to have so wonderful a day and so very dear a friend."

I felt righteous good seeing my two ladies looking at each other. And very happy knowing that Miss Kelly and Miss Boland would always be pals. Seeing the two of them sort of prodded me to look at Soup. He was smiling too.

So I punched him and he punched me back.

But then I felt a harder hand on my shoulder. Turning, I saw Mr. Carlotta. He also had collared Soup.

"Boys," he said, "it's decision time."

"Oh, *no,*" I heard Soup groan.

"And," said Mr. Carlotta, "I've decided that, instead of telling your parents how you stole my horse, the pair of you rascals will come back to my barn, and clean the manure out of every single stall."

"That's a lot of work," sighed Soup. But then, as Mr. Carlotta's hand tightened a mite, Soup added, "But we'll do it. Honest."

"Where's my horse?"

We showed him. But Mr. Carlotta let us ride Thunderbolt, at a slow walk, all the way over to his place. Two hours later, Soup and I were covered with horse dirt, not to mention at least a hundred flies, yet the stalls were finally cleaner than Sunday.

"You're learning," said Mr. Carlotta.

"You won't squeal on us?" Soup asked.

Mr. Carlotta smiled. "No, not this time. I was a kid once myself. And boys sometimes just *have* to be cowboys. So *git.* Unless you want more work. And take that old saddle with you."

"Yes, *sir*," I told him. "And thanks."

"I suppose," said Soup, as we were lugging the big saddle through the meadow, "we ought to drop it by the dump."

"But," I said, "I don't guess we will."

"Some stuff," said Soup, "is hard to let loose of."

I knew what he meant. An old cowboy saddle was sort of like a special teacher. And a very shiny day.

Worth keeping forever.

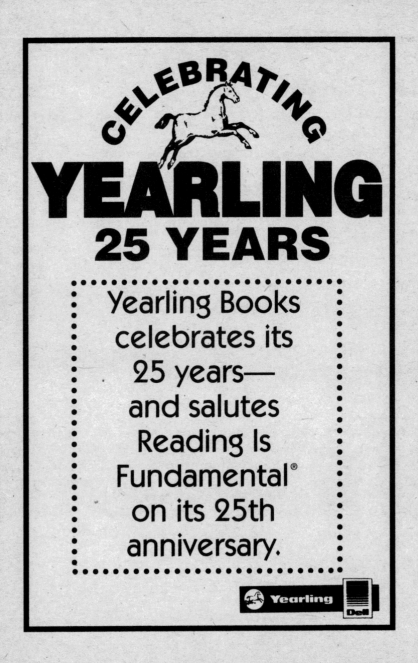

SOUP

RIDES AGAIN!

Whether he's riding into trouble on horseback or rolling into trouble on an outrageous set of wheels, Soup and his best friend Rob have a knack for the kind of crazy mix-ups that are guaranteed to make you laugh out loud!

☐ SOUP 48186-4 $2.95

☐ SOUP AND ME 48187-2 $2.95

☐ SOUP FOR PRESIDENT 48188-0 $2.50

☐ SOUP IN THE SADDLE 40032-5 $2.75

☐ SOUP ON FIRE 40193-3 $2.95

☐ SOUP ON ICE 40115-1 $2.75

☐ SOUP ON WHEELS 48190-2 $2.95

☐ SOUP'S DRUM.......................40003-1 $2.95

☐ SOUP'S GOAT.......................40130-5 $2.75

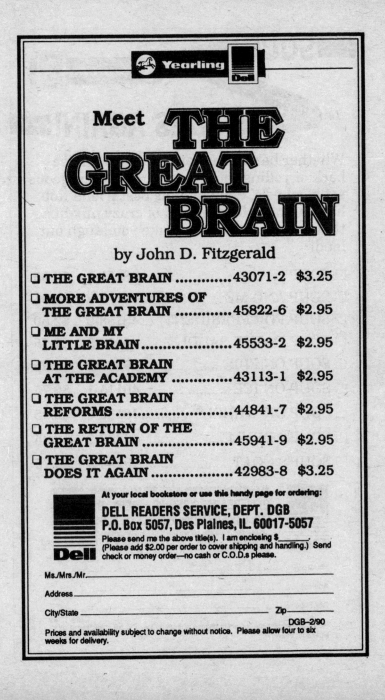